Bush Pilot!
Flying High Over Australia

Written by Robyn Brode
Illustrated by Paul Hayes

BARRON'S

First edition for the United States and Canada published exclusively by Barron's Educational Series, Inc. in 2002

Created and produced by Orange Avenue Publishing, Inc., San Francisco
© 2002 Orange Avenue Publishing, Inc.
Illustrations © 2002 Paul Hayes

All inquiries should be addressed to:
Barron's Educational Series, Inc.
250 Wireless Boulevard
Hauppauge, NY 11788
http://www.barronseduc.com

International Standard Book No. 0-7641-2153-7

Library of Congress Catalog Card No. 2001097897

Printed in Singapore
9 8 7 6 5 4 3 2 1

Bush Pilot!

Flying High Over Australia

AUSTRALIA

The flag of England appears in the top left corner of Australia's flag, because this country was discovered and primarily settled by people from England.

My dad is a **bush pilot**. He flies a small **bush plane** to remote areas in Australia, mostly in the **outback**.

We arrive early at the airport.
We have many miles to travel
today and quite a few packages
to deliver.

DID YOU KNOW?
A bush plane should be safe to land anywhere that's flat. It should also be easy to start and repair.

My dad puts gasoline in the gas tank. Then he makes sure everything is working the way it should.

DID YOU KNOW?

Bush pilots see where they're going by watching the land below them. They usually have no radio contact to guide them.

We climb into the plane, lock the doors, and fasten our seatbelts.

Up, up, and away!
High in the sky we go!

We see the red desert land of the outback spreading out for hundreds of miles below.

Look, there's something moving. It's a kangaroo! Maybe it's chasing the shadow of our plane.

DID YOU KNOW?

Sometimes a bush pilot is asked to fly someone to a hospital.

Today's first delivery is to a vet, an animal doctor. He needs what we bring him to do his job.

We see him waiting for us on his motorcycle. I think he's glad to see us.

We take off again from the dirt road we landed on. We make lots of dust!

DID YOU KNOW?
In the bush it is common to land on roads and fields — wherever it is hard and flat.

A **dingo** watches us, silent and still. Perhaps it thinks the plane is a bird as it rises in the sky.

We stop for lunch in a large, flat area that is dotted with eucalyptus trees.

A koala, high in a tree, is having lunch, too. Time to go! I wonder if it sees us as we fly overhead.

Our next stop is at a sheep ranch. We see a sheepherder on horseback, driving sheep back to the ranch.

We deliver some packages to the rancher. Look at all the wool — lots of sheep got haircuts!

Suddenly, off to the right in the distance, I see Ayers Rock, also called Uluru.

My dad says there are many rock paintings in the area. These petroglyphs were made by aboriginal peoples centuries ago.

Where did the time go? It is starting to get late, so my dad heads the plane toward home.

As we fly, I think about the miles we have flown and the places we have been — all in one day!

The sun is setting and soon it will be dark. At last, there's the airstrip. Down, down we go.

My dad parks the plane, then we head for home. It's been a long day, and we're tired and hungry.

Tonight, as I lie asleep in my bed, I dream that I am the pilot of my own bush plane.

I soar high and fly across the sky, delivering all sorts of things to all sorts of people!

SETTLEMENT

An English explorer, Captain James Cook, came upon the southeastern coast of Australia just over 230 years ago.

A few years later, England founded a colony there called New South Wales. The continent began to be called Australia about 100 years ago.

Most of the people sent from England to New South Wales were prisoners convicted of crimes.

Then gold was discovered about 150 years ago. People came from everywhere, and the number of people doubled!

Most people settled on the coast. Since Australia is a continent, there is a continuous coastline!

Other people began farming and raising sheep and cattle in the bush areas near the coast.

Few people live in the outback, the huge central area that gets little rain.

Northern Territory

Queensland

Western Australia

South Australia

New South Wales

Victoria

DID YOU KNOW?

Australia is the only place in the world where an entire continent is one country.

GLOSSARY

The Australian bush is any wild area that is outside a city. The bush is usually green or tropical. It is a place where you would like to go bushwalking (hiking).

A bush pilot flies a bush plane to all places that are a long way from cities. This includes many bush areas, such as where sheep are raised. But most faraway places in Australia are in the outback.

Away from the coast, three-fourths of Australia becomes the outback. Few people or animals live in the outback, a flat inland desert of red soil and rock.

Female kangaroos are most famous for their pouch (pocket), in which they grow and carry one baby at a time. They only eat plants, and like to sit on their long, thick tails. Kangaroos are only found in Australia.

In the Australian outback, it is common to see medium-sized wild dogs, which are called dingoes. They only live in Australia.

Eucalyptus trees are native to Australia. They are always green and grow very tall. Lots of animals like to eat their berries and leaves.

Koalas look like little bears, but they're definitely not. They live in eucalyptus trees — food is always close to home. Koalas make their home only in Australia.

Petroglyphs are old drawings, carvings, or writings made on rocks. Petro stands for rock, so perhaps we should call today's wall writings petrograffiti!

Aboriginals or aborigines means original people. Aboriginals have lived in Australia for about 40,000 years. They continue to live in Australia, although now other people live there, too.

The books in the **Going Places** series are produced by Orange Avenue, Inc.

Creative Director: **Hallie Warshaw**
Writer: **Robyn Brode** • Designer: **Britt Menendez**
Illustrator: **Paul Hayes** • Coordinator and researcher: **Emily Vassos**
Photos: **Corbis, Eyewire, Getty and Picturequest**

Thanks to:
Amanda Wilkinson and **Tom Claytor**,
Australian bush pilots

Original concept for series:
Hallie Warshaw and
Mark Shulman